2010

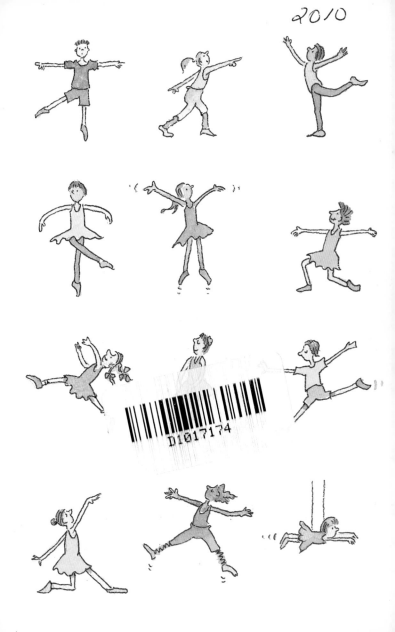

Ladybird

This Little Story
belongs to

_____

Published by Ladybird Books Ltd
27 Wrights Lane London W8 5TZ
A Penguin Company
3 5 7 9 10 8 6 4

Illustrations © David Pace MCMXCVII
© LADYBIRD BOOKS LTD MCMXCVII

Printed in Italy

Daisy, Little Dancer

by Marie Birkinshaw
illustrated by David Pace

Daisy loved to dance. More than anything else she wanted to be a famous ballet dancer. Every night she dreamed of performing in front of a real audience.

But today was Daisy's first lesson at her new dancing school. As she walked into the huge hall, she felt a little worried.

"Hello, Daisy," said Mrs Pringle, the dancing teacher. Daisy thought Mrs Pringle looked beautiful – elegant, tall and graceful.

Then Daisy met the other dancers in the class. They had all been to the school before. Daisy was the only new one there and she was by far the smallest dancer in the hall. Now Daisy began to feel very worried indeed.

Daisy looked round at the other dancers, warming up ready for the lesson to begin.

She could see Selina and Sophie, admiring themselves in the mirror. They were so tall and slender.

Then there was a small group of dancers, exercising at the barre.

Suddenly, three boys came rushing across the room and nearly knocked Daisy over. They were the Noisy Trio, as Mrs Pringle called them – Nigel, Dan and Andrew.

"Whoops! Sorry!" Nigel said to Daisy. "You're so small, we didn't see you."

Whoops! Sorry!

"Listen now, everyone!" called Mrs Pringle. "This summer I would like this class to perform *The Silver Swan*, and you will ALL take part."

Everyone cheered. They had all heard of *The Silver Swan*. The costumes were great, and the music was brilliant with lots of drums, trumpets and tinkling chimes.

Daisy wasn't sure what it was, but she felt excited all the same.

"This morning," said Mrs Pringle, "I should like to choose who will play which part. We will start with the trees. Listen to the music for the wind in the trees, and watch carefully!"

Mrs Pringle waved her arms and danced on the spot. She looked just like a beautiful tree swaying in the breeze.

SWISH! SWISH! SWISH! SWISH!

"Now it's your turn!" said
Mrs Pringle.

The dancers waved their arms and
danced on the spot.

SWISH! SWISH! SWISH! SWISH!

Mrs Pringle chose Selina and
Sophie to be the trees...

but she didn't choose Daisy.

Isn't Mrs Pringle lovely!

"Next," said Mrs Pringle, "I want you to dance like fire! Listen to the music for the flames, and watch carefully."

Mrs Pringle danced towards Selina and Sophie. Her arms leapt out like fiery flames, around the slender trees.

FLICKER!

FLICKER!

CRACKLE!

CRACKLE!

"Now it's your turn!" said
Mrs Pringle.

The dancers leapt round the hall
like raging fire.

FLICKER! FLICKER!
CRACKLE! CRACKLE!

"Very good!" said Mrs Pringle, and
she chose the Noisy Trio to be the
flames...

but she didn't choose Daisy.

"Now," called Mrs Pringle, tapping her stick for attention, "I want you to pretend to be woodland creatures, running away from the flames. Listen to the music for the creatures running, and watch carefully."

Mrs Pringle ran away from the Noisy Trio like a frightened animal.

SWOOSH! SWOOSH!
SCAMPER! SCAMPER!

"Now it's your turn!" she said.

Everyone danced their very best.

SWOOSH! SWOOSH!
SCAMPER! SCAMPER!

Mrs Pringle chose the rest of the dancers to be the woodland creatures…

but she didn't choose Daisy!

Daisy was the only dancer without a part. She wanted to cry.

"Now," said Mrs Pringle, "I would usually choose an older dancer for the star role, but this year I have decided to do something a little different. The Silver Swan will fly across the stage on dancers' ropes. For this we need the smallest and lightest dancer in the school."

Everyone looked at Daisy.

I bet I know who it is!

"I know this is your very first lesson, Daisy," Mrs Pringle said, "but I wonder if you would like to be the Silver Swan?"

Daisy was thrilled. "Me!" she gasped. "Oh, Mrs Pringle, I'd love to!"

So the ropes were tied round Daisy's waist, and she swept across the stage.

Daisy's class practised really hard that summer. At the end of term, they put on the special performance of *The Silver Swan*. And everyone came to see it…

The curtain rose and the musicians began to play.

SWISH! SWISH! SWISH! SWISH!

The trees swayed in the breeze. But the wind grew stronger… and stronger.

Suddenly there was a loud crack, as lightning struck the trees and flames leapt around them.

FLICKER! FLICKER!
CRACKLE! CRACKLE!

Those flames are noisy, aren't they?

I'm so proud!

The woodland creatures started
to flee.

SWOOSH! SWOOSH!

SCAMPER! SCAMPER!

They were terrified and didn't know
where to go. Just then the animals
looked up. There above them,
swooping softly and silently, was the
Silver Swan. *She* would show them
to safety.

And Daisy, the little dancer, glided gently before them and led the woodland creatures safely to the Silver Lagoon…

Everyone clapped and cheered and shouted for more.

The musicians and dancers had done so well that Mrs Pringle wanted to cry for joy.

Daisy was the proudest *little* dancer in the whole ballet school. Perhaps one day she would be famous, after all…